The
Binky
Mouse
Series

Published by Nomedigas Publishing
nomedigaspublishing@gmail.com

Author's website
www.binkymouse.com

ISBN 978-1-52362-8131

Also available as a Kindle ebook
ISBN 978-1-84396-395-0

Pre-press production
eBook Versions
27 Old Gloucester Street, London WC1N 3AX
www.ebookversions.com

Binky Mouse
and the
Music Man

Sheila Hoeman

Can you count Binky's buttons?

Once upon a time there was a mouse called

Binky Mouse

Binky Mouse was a furry, brown mouse who lived on the edge of an allotment. He was a very smart mouse. He had a T-shirt with 12 buttons. He had some trousers with stripes going up and down and across.

He had two furry little ears and a happy smile.

Binky Mouse lived in a house under the ground. It had a door made of grass that went up as you went in and a floor made of straw. It had a yellow carpet with a flowery pattern and a sofa.

It had a bed covered with patterns of cheese and a matchbox for his toys at the bottom of the bed.

Where do your toys live?

Who do you like to visit?

There were pictures of cheese all around the wall and some photos of his family.

Binky Mouse had a cheese boxing bag to keep fit and some fruit in a cabbage leaf on the table. There was a book called "How to get away from a cat trap" that he read every night.

He also had a best friend called Blot. Binky and Blot liked to have adventures. They liked to visit each other as their houses were so different.

Blot lived in a house near a railway station. It was very noisy and dark. It had a door made of an old cloth bag that used to have newspapers in it.

Blot loved to read and his dark little house was full of books that he had made from bits of newspapers. These books were all about how the world worked, including what made wheels turn. Blot always wanted the answer to everything and he used his books to help him find out.

Can you find an information book?

How do you keep fit?

Binky liked to keep fit by eating healthy food and exercising. He liked to help Blot keep fit and Blot liked to keep Binky informed about the world, so they had a very good friendship.

One day Binky and Blot were jogging through the railway station's pedestrian tunnel when they saw the music man sitting all on his own looking very sad.

He usually played his saxophone to the people travelling on the trains. If they liked his music they would give him money to buy his dinner

Today the music man was sad and hungry because he couldn't make any music come out of his saxophone. When he blew down the tube no music came out.

Can you make an instrument?

Which smells do you like?

Binky and Blot scratched their furry little ears. "It must be blocked," said Blot. "Come on Binky, let's have a look." The music man put his saxophone on the ground.

Binky and Blot had a good sniff first. They wiggled their whiskers and Binky crawled inside the slippery, cold tube. Blot was still sniffing. He thought he could smell something familiar but he couldn't quite think what it was.

As they skittered along, Binky whispered, "Cheese – I smell cheese!" Blot nodded. Of course, that's what the smell was, but how could a saxophone smell of cheese?

Binky tried to go faster but he slipped and rolled over and over in the dark tube. Blot could see the stripes on his trousers making patterns in the air – it made him feel quite dizzy.

Can you make some stripey patterns?

Can you play an instrument?

But then he started sliding too. He tumbled into Binky, who was lying on something soft and squashy with a very yummy smell.

It was a cheese sandwich! Some silly traveller had eaten most of his sandwich and then thrown the last of it away. It had landed in the music man's saxophone and had wedged in the tube.

That was what was stopping the music coming out! The air couldn't get through the tube when the music man blew.

Binky and Blot soon put that right. "Dinner!" squeaked Binky and the two friends munched their way happily through the cheese sandwich until it had quite gone – not even a crumb was left!

What do you like to eat?

Can you listen to some saxophone music?

Just then the music man decided to try his sax again – and before they could say "Kitty-cats" the two friends were sailing through the air, followed by a booming note from the sax and a happy chuckle from the music man. Now he could eat too.

Binky and Blot picked themselves up from the corner of the railway station's pedestrian tunnel where they'd landed. As they shook themselves clean, the music man waved happily at them and they scampered off to Blot's house to read his books on musical instruments and to plan their next adventure.

Can you find a book for your friend?

Printed in Great Britain
by Amazon